Dear Parent:

Your child's love of reading starts here!

Every child learns to read in a different way and at his or her own speed. Some go back and forth between reading levels and read favorite books again and again. Others read through each level in order. You can help your young reader improve and become more confident by encouraging his or her own interests and abilities. From books your child reads with you to the first books he or she reads alone, there are I Can Read Books for every stage of reading:

SHARED READING
Basic language, word repetition, and whimsical illustrations, ideal for sharing with your emergent reader

BEGINNING READING
Short sentences, familiar words, and simple concepts for children eager to read on their own

READING WITH HELP
Engaging stories, longer sentences, and language play for developing readers

READING ALONE
Complex plots, challenging vocabulary, and high-interest topics for the independent reader

I Can Read Books have introduced children to the joy of reading since 1957. Featuring award-winning authors and illustrators and a fabulous cast of beloved characters, I Can Read Books set the standard for beginning readers.

A lifetime of discovery begins with the magical words **"I Can Read!"**

*Visit www.icanread.com for information
on enriching your child's reading experience.*

I Can Read!

BEGINNING READING 1

Pinkalicious®

Kittens! Kittens! Kittens!

To Whitepaws, Greypaws, Abra, Sting,
Nellie, Gustavo, Blue, Belle, and to all the
purrrrfect feline friends that we have
known and continue to love.
—V.K.

The author gratefully acknowledges
the artistic and editorial contributions of
Daniel Griffo and Jacqueline Resnik.

I Can Read® and I Can Read Book® are trademarks of HarperCollins Publishers.

Pinkalicious: Kittens! Kittens! Kittens!
Copyright © 2024 by VBK., Co.

PINKALICIOUS and all related logos are trademarks of VBK, Co. Used with permission.

LLibrary of Congress Control Number: 2023937531
ISBN 978-0-06-325735-1 (trade bdg.) — ISBN 978-0-06-325734-4 (pbk.)

24 25 26 27 CWM 10 9 8 7 6 5 4 3 2

First Edition

I Can Read!

BEGINNING 1 READING

Pinkalicious®

Kittens! Kittens! Kittens!

by Victoria Kann

HARPER
An Imprint of HarperCollinsPublishers

My family was fostering
a cuterrific cat named Tiger
while the animal shelter
was under renovation.

Tiger was big and sweet.

She moved slowly.

"She seems tired," Peter said.

"Being here is a big change for her,"
Mommy said.

"Maybe you are sleepy?"

I asked Tiger.

She purred in response.

I carried the big cat to her bed.

"Good night, Tiger!" I said.

The next morning, I heard a meow.

"Meow, meow, meow, meow.

Meow, meow, meow."

A lot of meows.

I sat up in bed.

I blinked.

I rubbed my eyes.

Tiger was surrounded by

the most pinkadorable kittens

I'd ever seen!

"Peter!" I yelled.

"Come quick!"

Peter came running.

"COLORRIFIC KITTENS?!" he said.

Mommy and Daddy hurried in.

"Oh my!" Mommy said.

"Now we know why

Tiger was so tired."

"It looks like we're now taking

care of seven cats!" Daddy said.

13

"Let's name the kittens!" I said.

"Don't get too attached," Mommy said.

"They are only living with us
until the animal shelter reopens."

"That's Sherbet and Scribbles,
and that's Checkers," I said.
"And Zigzag and Stripes!"
Peter added.
"And you are Pinkadot!"
I said to the pinkacutest kitten.

Having kittens was pinkamazing.

Every week they got more fun.

Week one: they were so tiny!

Week three: they could stand on

their own!

By week five: PLAYTIME!

"Can we please keep one kitten?"
I asked Mommy and Daddy.
"I'll help take care of it,"
Peter said.

"No," Daddy said.

"Kittens are too much work."

"Pinkaplease?" I begged.

"I'm sorry," Mommy said.

"We can't," Daddy said.

That night at bedtime,

I found Peter in his room

with the kittens.

"I want to keep one,"

he said with a sniffle.

I gave Peter a hug.

"Me too," I said.

"If we help take care of them,
maybe Mommy and Daddy
will change their minds!"

Every day the kittens were
getting bigger and more active.
"Look, Pinkalicious!" said Peter
one morning.

"It's kitten chaos!" I said.

"What a mess."

"Oh no!" Mommy said.

"This is why we can't keep a kitten!"

Peter and I worked hard cleaning up.

To thank us, Daddy cooked

our favorite foods.

"Dinner à la Daddy is ready!"

he said.

Chef Daddy led us into the kitchen.

"Tonight we will be having—

MESSY MEATBALLS?!" he said.

"I guess the kittens

like my cooking!"

"This is a cat-astrophe!" I said
as Peter and I cleaned up again.
"We'll never get a kitten now,"
Peter said sadly.

We went to the couch.

The kittens cuddled with us.

Sherbet nuzzled Peter.

I kissed Pinkadot's tiny pink nose.

"I love you, Pinkadot," I said.

"The kittens are sweet when they
aren't making a mess," Mommy said.
"Can't we can't keep just one?"
I pleaded.
"You both have been very helpful
and have cleaned up their messes..."
Mommy said.

"Well . . ." Daddy said.

Pinkadot licked Daddy.

"Maybe just one," they agreed.

"Which kitten should
we adopt?" Mommy asked.

Pinkadot jumped into my arms.

"I think we have our answer,"
Daddy said with a laugh.

"KITTENTASTIC!" Peter and I cheered.

It turned out we weren't the only
family getting a new pet.
When the shelter reopened,
everyone wanted some kittens!

The kittens all had new homes,

and we had a purrrfect new pet.

"Pinkadot is the pinkabest!" I said.